POETRY MONSTERS

Fangtastic Poets

Edited By Kat Cockrill

First published in Great Britain in 2020 by:

YoungWriters® Est. 1991

Young Writers
Remus House
Coltsfoot Drive
Peterborough
PE2 9BF
Telephone: 01733 890066
Website: www.youngwriters.co.uk

All Rights Reserved
Book Design by Ashley Janson
© Copyright Contributors 2019
Softback ISBN 978-1-83928-773-2

Printed and bound in the UK by BookPrintingUK
Website: www.bookprintinguk.com
YB0432O

FOREWORD

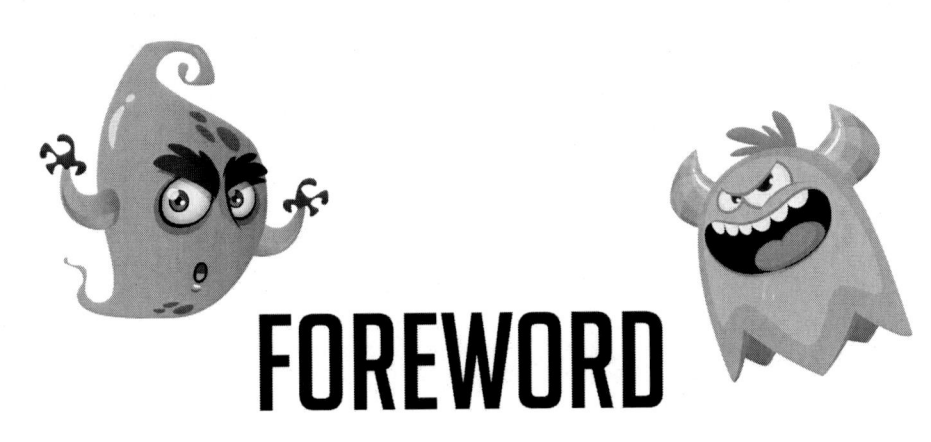

Hello Reader!

For our latest poetry competition we sent out funky and vibrant worksheets for primary school pupils to fill in and create their very own poem about fiendish fiends and crazy creatures. I got to read them and guess what? They were **roarsome**!

The pupils were able to read our example poems and use the fun-filled free resources to help bring their imaginations to life, and the result is pages **oozing** with exciting poetic tales. From friendly monsters to mean monsters, from bumps in the night to **rip-roaring** adventures, these pupils have excelled themselves, and now have the joy of seeing their work in print!

Here at Young Writers we love nothing more than poetry and creativity. We aim to encourage children to put pen to paper to inspire a love of the written word and explore their own unique worlds of creativity. We'd like to congratulate all of the aspiring authors that have created this book of **monstrous mayhem** and we know that these poems will be enjoyed for years to come. So, dive on in and submerge yourself in all things furry and fearsome (and perhaps check under the bed!).

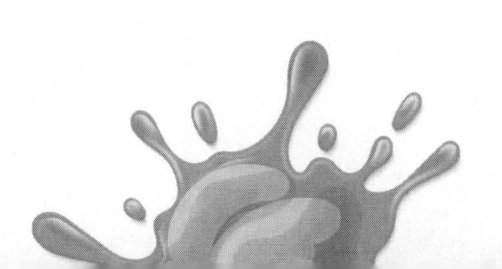

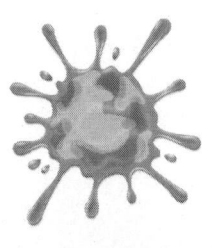

CONTENTS

All Saints Primary School, Greenock

Niah Carlin (7)	1
Kayden Barr (8)	2
Lucy Wilson (8)	3
Millie Charlotte Green (7)	4
Peyton McFadyen (6)	5
Oliver Paul Weston (8)	6
Peyton Anderson (7)	7
Ava Casement (8)	8
Edward Joyce (7)	9
Jude Thomas Rodger Donnachie (8)	10
Roman Boyle (8)	11
Charley McDonald (7)	12

Broad Heath Community Primary School, Coventry

Humza Habib (10)	13
Ayesha Gray (10)	14
Sean Dhanda (10)	18
Amelia Mathews (10)	20
Leeda Daud (10)	22
Leona May Donal (11)	23
Mahamad Yousif (11)	24
Leena Naziri (11)	25
Sariya Hassan (10)	26
Anya Dahoo (10)	27
Jamie Grant-Hall (10)	28
Zara Hussain (10)	29

Buxlow Preparatory School, Wembley

Kianna Pabari (11)	30
Megu Mizuno (7)	31
Raihan Ahmed (10)	32
Noor Al-Zahra Al-Saraj (9)	33
Amelia Khan (11)	34
Ruth Emma Caraiman (8)	35
Amelia Campbell (10)	36
Eesa Gaffar (7)	37
Tara Razban (7)	38
Timi Areoye (9)	39
Sofia Humayun (8)	40
Danyaal Kirmani (8)	41
Nasma Nagi Karileamiden (9)	42
Elias Humayun (7)	43

Eureka Primary School, Midway

Samuel Epworth (9)	44
Corey Barrett-Gray (10)	45
Boglarka Hegedus (10)	46
Caolan Devitt (10)	47
Makenzie Tilt (10)	48

Georgetown Primary School, Tredegar

Isabella Hill (9)	49
Tilly Jones (10)	50
Isabella Templer (9)	52
Mia Kerri Smith (10)	54
Evan Howells (9)	55
Emily Howells (9)	56

Kent College Junior School, Harbledown

Rebecca Temple-Masters (10)	57
Liza Molkova (8)	58
Poppy Armstrong (11)	60
Katie Wilkinson (10)	61
Jim Littlechild (7)	62
Jake Jennings (7)	63

Lathom Junior School, East Ham

Ayan Kazi (7)	64
Sasmeya Jeyatharsan (7)	66
Azaan Muhammed (7)	67
Romman Ali (8)	68
Yaafi Muhamed Kalil (7)	69
Azha Aboobucker (8)	70
Basit Shazhad (7)	71

Richmond Avenue Primary School, Shoeburyness

Elena Rose Skehan (7)	72
Maisy Mulligan (7)	73
Bethany Rayner (7)	74
Chaye Franklin (7)	75
Jack Nicholls (7)	76
Lily Scrafton (7)	77
Sidney Davis (7)	78
Frederick Strydom (8)	79
Olly Owens (8)	80
Isla Mayne (7)	81
Leah Rudkin (7)	82
Helena Reilly (7)	83
Henry Gibbs (7)	84
Roi Reeves (7)	85
Phoebe Vickers (7)	86
Henry James Peek (7)	87
Emily Hayes (8)	88
Maisie-leigh Ann Craven (7)	89
Roody Gregory (8)	90
Edward Davis (7)	91
Finley Moyser (8)	92

Amber Queen-Brooks (7)	93
Amelie Ellen Morley (7)	94
Maxx Mulligan (7)	95
Eliza Grooms (7)	96
Tommy Heal (7)	97
Teddy Rutt (8)	98
Daniel Floyd (7)	99
Harley Adams (7)	100
Mason Osborne (7)	101
Matthew Bannister (7)	102
Anna Rayner (7)	103
Luqa James (8)	104
Summer Nunn (8)	105
Ava-Mai Westaway (6)	106

Ripponden Junior & Infant School, Ripponden

Martha Faye Valentine Appleby (9)	107
Isla Alice Vevers (10) & Maya Rose Willacy	108
Annabella Brook (10)	110
Amelie Wallwork (10)	112
Alisha Whitelaw (9)	113
Willow Jennings (10)	114
Gwynneth Harrison-Walker (11)	115
Ben Lucas Hillcoat (8)	116
George Hughes (10)	117
Eryn Ideson-Sharp (11)	118
Sophie Oxley (9)	119
Else Hughes (8)	120
Poppy Sowden (9)	121
Katie Huckauf (9)	122
Freya Elizabeth Gatehouse (9)	123
Gioia Giardina (8)	124
Charlotte Mae Wood (8)	125
Poppy Laws (10) & Lucy Hood (10)	126
Evan Jacob Leyland (9)	127
Cameron William Snape (9)	128

Tai Education Centre, Penygraig

Kenny Jenkins (9)	129
Jack Swales (9)	130
Kian Davies (10)	131
Cameron Williams (10)	132

Uffculme Primary School, Uffculme

Lottie Watson (7)	133
Maisy Whitehead (7)	134
Alfie Craig Collins (7)	136
Zac Matthews (8)	137
Flora Copland (8)	138
Kara Kneale (8)	139
Laurie Poynton (7)	140
Jack Bolt (8)	141
Amelia Emma Anne Hanley (7)	142
Harry Johnson (8)	143
Kian Hector (8)	144
Alyssia Irene Hayes (7)	145
Jagoda Kramarz (8)	146
Louis Taylor (7)	147
Wiktoria Bylicka (7)	148
Harley Carreau (8)	149
Freya C H Mills (7)	150
Maddox Welch (7)	151
Summer Freeman (7)	152
Alfie Ibbitson (7)	153
Alfie Tarr (8)	154
Jacob Jaffri (8)	155
Kayla Pike (8)	156
Taylor Lindsell (8)	157
Declan Hutchings (7)	158
Isaac Ronnie Tanner (8)	159
Fyfe Milby (8)	160
Mike Orchard (7)	161
Emilie Matthews (9)	162
Koby Ware (8)	163

Victoria Road Primary School, Ashford

Agata Julianna Bolejko (6)	164

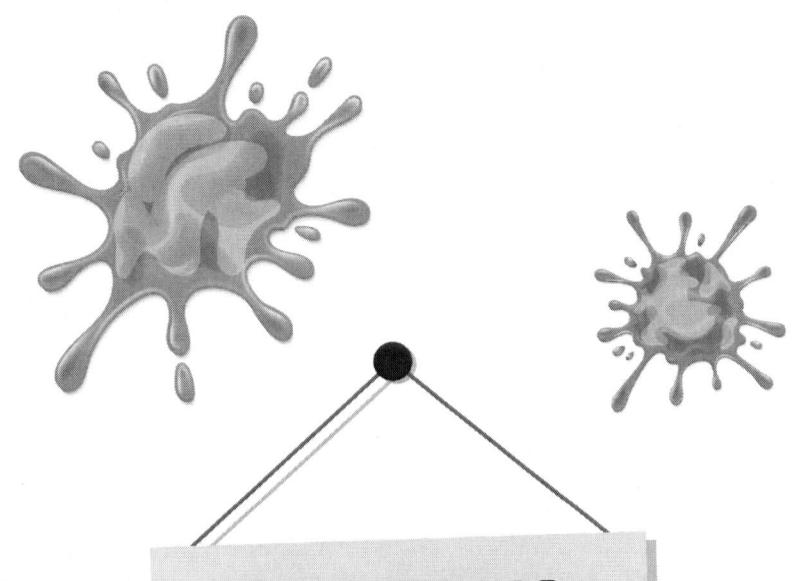

THE POEMS

The Bloody Vampire

My monster is a fierce vampire
It is as bloody as a dead cheetah
And as evil as a really bad wizard
It is like a gorilla, so big
And it is like a wizard
My monster is black and scary
It is bloody and spiky
When I look at it,
It looks at me scarily and it is big
I would take my monster to a coffin
I would feed my monster blood
I am friends with my monster
It is fierce.

Niah Carlin (7)
All Saints Primary School, Greenock

The Fiercest Werewolf

My monster is a werewolf
It is as scary as a vampire
And as greedy as an alligator
It is as stinky as cheese, mouldy and ugly
My monster is grey and spiky
It is bloody and has sharp teeth
When I say "Snap!" it breaks a tree
I would take my monster to a football game
I would feed my monster blood and guts
I am friends with my monster
It is fierce.

Kayden Barr (8)
All Saints Primary School, Greenock

The Vampire Princess

My monster is a Vampire Princess
It is as scary as a ghost
And as spooky as an evil zombie
It is an evil princess, pretty and moany,
My monster is white and it has feathers
It is cold-hearted and it has wings
When I see it, it jumps and giggles
I would take my monster to a party
I would feed my monster cakes
I am scared of my monster
It is terrifying.

Lucy Wilson (8)
All Saints Primary School, Greenock

Evil Ghost Vampire

My monster is a ghost vampire
It is as greedy as a dinosaur
And as fast as a flash
It is as stinky as a sock, funny and ugly,
My monster is clear and scary
It has feathers and is angry
When I pat it, it jumps and it is happy
I would take my monster to a football game
I would feed my monster a taco
I am not friends with my monster
It is evil.

Millie Charlotte Green (7)
All Saints Primary School, Greenock

The Evil Witch Monster

My monster is an evil witch
She has the powers of a sorceress
She made herself fast as lightning
Her skin is green, slimy and glittering, frightening

My monster has a roar as fierce as a lion
She eats stinky cheese and macaroni
Her only friend is a scary pony

My monster lives in a dark, mouldy cave
She loves to come out to give a wave.

Peyton McFadyen (6)
All Saints Primary School, Greenock

The Fearless Chocolate

My monster is a red chocolate bar
It is as fearless as a football
And as fast as a polar bear
It is a giant chocolate bar, ugly and melty
My monster is spiky and red
It is angry and slimy
When I touch it, it moves and roars
I would take my monster to Tesco
I would feed my monster dead fish
I am friends with my monster
It is evil.

Oliver Paul Weston (8)
All Saints Primary School, Greenock

The Creepy Pebble

My monster is a creepy pebble
It is as fast as a lightning bolt
As scary as a killer clown
And as greedy as a big bear
It is like a really, really fast cheetah,
Angry and spiky
My monster is white and spiky
It is fluffy and angry
When I tickle it, it giggles and dances
I would take my monster to a creepy cinema.

Peyton Anderson (7)
All Saints Primary School, Greenock

Zombie Cheerleader

My monster is a zombie
It is as scary as a dragon
And as greedy as a shark
It is a boulder, smelly and crazy
It is moany and big
When I play with it, it giggles and jumps
I would take my monster to a monster park
I would feed my monster eyeball soup
I am friends with my monster
It is very scary.

Ava Casement (8)
All Saints Primary School, Greenock

Monster Legend

My monster is a ghost
It is as scary as a zombie and as dark as a crow
It is a pig, greedy and fat
My monster is blue and slimy
It is spiky and angry
When I feed it, it jumps and giggles
I would take my monster to a cave
I feed my monster apples
I am friends with my monster
It is happy.

Edward Joyce (7)
All Saints Primary School, Greenock

Devil

The devil is evil
And he can turn into fire
That exists even in the rain
He is tougher than steel
He is red
If you look really close to his eyes
You will see fire burning away
The devil has a sword that cuts
Through anything
He even makes the Gods scared.

Jude Thomas Rodger Donnachie (8)
All Saints Primary School, Greenock

The Werewolf

My monster is a werewolf
It is as fast as a cheetah
And as smelly as a bin
It is an evil monster and as vicious as a lion
My monster is black and spiky
It is angry and cold-blooded
When I feed it, it jumps up and down
I would like to take my monster to a volcano.

Roman Boyle (8)
All Saints Primary School, Greenock

The Princess Vampire

My monster is a princess vampire
It is as dark as a dark scary cave
And as scary as a killer clown
It is as greedy as a big, fat bear
My monster is black and soft
It is fluffy and scary
When I feed it, it jumps and screams.

Charley McDonald (7)
All Saints Primary School, Greenock

The Silent Devil

In the dark days of doom, beware the monster
The one called Silencer, the one that's sneaky
He lurks in the shadows, his real name is Conner
He is very criminal and cheeky

He has two bodyguards, they have a Freezer Ray
Silencer is a dummy and made form clay
He is destroying souls and he can't go away
"You have the right to remain silent," he'd just say

Silencer plays with his victims, creating chaos
Tricks them dares them all sorts
When the day of doom comes, he is the boss
At the time Freezer Ray appears they run full courts

He is demanding to his bodyguards, help him slay!
He is evil to his targets to keep him in his place
He may never go which means he is here today...

Humza Habib (10)
Broad Heath Community Primary School, Coventry

Murder At Midnight

Maria was a monster, fierce as could be
Her roars and growl were spine-tingling as anyone could see
Although her looks suggested otherwise
She was a big softie in disguise

However, every time she sat brushing her shrunken head
She cried with sorrow in the bed
"I will curse my brother for what he did!"
And you should know she was not one to kid

Maria was the monster of sewage
On the toilet, she would drag you down
Where you would meet your doom and drown

Then her brother wrote a song
And it went a bit, well, exactly like this
Little did he know it would bring the misery of an abyss

"My sister Maria
She got diarrhoea
She did a poo in bed

Then she did a big fart
That would stop your heart..."
Well I could carry on
But there would be no point
For Maria's brother was screaming
In pain as Maria snapped his joints

That was it, Maria was on a rage
She was on a wild killing sage
Her fangs came out
Her eyes bright red
Slash, bang, claw
Another head!

This was it, Maria calmed down
Yet she was still sitting with a stern frown
She plonked herself down on the bed
Whilst licking the blood from her shrunken head

These are the next words she said,
"You will pay for this brother dear,
The time is coming
The end is near
Enjoy your last moments of your life

For the very last will bring you pain and strife!"

So now we're back to the present time
Maria's waiting for the clock to chime
Her white fangs are gleaming with pride
Quick, she's coming, hide, hide, hide!

Maria's brother Sedrick walked past
She pounced on him stealthily and took him down fast
He squirmed and squiggled
Rolled and wriggled
Yet he couldn't break free
"Ha!" screamed Maria. "It's me!"

Sedrick begged Maria he even pleaded
A second chance was all he needed

But Maria was sure this is what she wanted to do
Just one pressing question, how? The loo!
So of course, as sisters tend to do
Sedrick met his sticky end, and drowned in poo!

This just goes to show never disrespect your sister
No, no, no!

Or you too could meet your smelly end
So never drive your sister round the bend.

Ayesha Gray (10)
Broad Heath Community Primary School, Coventry

The Monsters Within Us...

We stopped looking for the monsters inside us, thus,
We then realised they were actually inside us
It might sound ridiculous and insane
But it feels like I am bound by a chain

He is the one concealing inside my head
Teeth razor-sharp and eyes gleaming red
He is killing me, why doesn't anyone care
Fingers like snakes and spiders in my hair

He plays the fool with the tear-away face
Here for a second, then leaves without a single trace
Drags his nails across the brick wall
Slender-like figure thin, yet tall

He is thirsty for fear and as deadly as the plague
His wrath no human can escape
From the snap of his finger, he can cause an explosion
His heart is full of stone and made of molten

He is in the shadows under moon
Every evening he sings its frightful little tune
At midnight when I'm fast asleep
On the spur of the moment, I hear a creep

He is always frightening and terrifying me
From the depths of my heart hear my pleas
Now that I lay my head down to sleep...
For I am begging the Lord for my life to keep.

Sean Dhanda (10)
Broad Heath Community Primary School, Coventry

Bleb Plans His Meal

It was a snowy winter's night and all the kids were sleeping
The lamp posts were watching out to see if Bleb was creeping
The bushes were crouching in the cold, wet breeze, huddling together, trying not to freeze
Bleb was hiding in the wardrobe ready to come out
Peeking through the gap to make sure no one was about
He was excited about tonight
Ready for his meal
There were three children to eat in this house
As long as the first one doesn't squeal
He thought about his plan
And the snacks he had in store
He was imagining all the flavours of the kids he'd eaten before
As he was preparing to make his gruesome attack
The nosy mum came in the room and gave him a good hard whack
"Go away, filthy beast, leave my kids alone, now go, don't come back, you're not welcome in my home!"

Bleb ran to the wardrobe and through his magic door
Never to be seen again, the monster was no more.

Amelia Mathews (10)
Broad Heath Community Primary School, Coventry

My Sleep Paralysis Demon

It's so quiet but everyone's screaming
I scratch myself but I think I'm dreaming
I don't feel anything but I'm bleeding
I'm cautiously running but I am not leaving
You showed me things I've never seen
Disturbed emotion, I never felt
Created anxiety with the thought of sleep
Made me fear the process of transition
Who are you?
You're my Sleep Paralysis Demon
Kept me awake, struck by the bloody moon
Besieged by your gaze, sunken spirit
Spying 'neath space, pallid face
Predatory eyes, pricking horns, buried skin deep
Cannot seize the day, no carpe diem
Tossing in my bed, drowned in endless requiem
My Sleep Paralysis Demon!

Leeda Daud (10)
Broad Heath Community Primary School, Coventry

Beware Of The Slime

My teacher Miss Harrison gave me a cup
I took the ingredients and mixed them all up

"Quick take a look."
Right there in the cup was a big pile of slime

The slime felt all squishy and gooey and smooth
I looked at it carefully... I'm sure it just moved

Then out of my hands crept the slime in a rush
And it landed on the floor like a big pile of mush

Quickly the slime oozed right across the floor
It slithered and stretched and escaped out the door

I tried to chase after The Slime Monster
But he was too fast
"Shall we try that again?" Miss Harrison asked.

Leona May Donal (11)
Broad Heath Community Primary School, Coventry

The Creation Of The Olympians

Retaliator is his name
He has it for a reason
On his head is a pink scarlet mane
He likes the winter season
Retaliator seeps through the darkness
He always shines bright like a star
He never needs a harness
Retaliator is faster than a sports car

Forged in the depths of Hephaestus' volcano
Hatched within Poseidon's palace
He doesn't have a glowing halo
Hermes gave him his malice

Retaliator is his name
He has it for a reason.

Mahamad Yousif (11)
Broad Heath Community Primary School, Coventry

Three Scary Monsters

Three scary monsters wandering around
Finds a friend's house and get ideas
They plan to scare and frighten some pests
Crash, smash, bye goes the windows

Scream, screech, shout, "Ahh!"
Monsters go in and wreak more stuff
But no one makes a noise
Monsters break bigger things

They still can't hear anything
They look around
And up and down
But still can't find anything

It is a mystery for them.

Leena Naziri (11)
Broad Heath Community Primary School, Coventry

Death At Night!

The wind howls in the night
The monster is out of sight
I went to bed
To rest my head
The following day
I just had to say
It was in front of me
Can't you see?
Its jaws were ready
Indeed, very steady
All I saw was red
'Cause I was dead!
So who else will it get?
We've never met
Beware!
It will catch a glimpse of your hair
You will be trapped in a cage
Shouting with rage!

Sariya Hassan (10)
Broad Heath Community Primary School, Coventry

Monsters

M aliciousness is in the air
O ozing lava in his volcano lair
N obody will survive
S niffing every corner of your street, looking for prey
T usks like an elephant
E erie sounds coming from the mouth that will end you
R ed, googly eyes stalking you while you sleep
S o beware of the monsters!

Anya Dahoo (10)
Broad Heath Community Primary School, Coventry

The Mech-Monster Strikes

Stomp, stomp, stomp!
The Mech-Monster came to town
Stomp, stomp, stomp!
The Mech-Monster cannot be beaten

Hide in your closet
As the buildings go down
Hide in your closet
Because the Mech-Monster has come to town!

Jamie Grant-Hall (10)
Broad Heath Community Primary School, Coventry

Fizzy The Monster

Fizzy the monster,
Who loves dusters
He loves fizzy drinks
And always winks

Fizzy the monster
Who has a brother called Oscar
And needs to go to the doctor
As he is really unhealthy.

Zara Hussain (10)
Broad Heath Community Primary School, Coventry

Fantastic Frantic

F amiliar as anyone can be
A nnoying but a fun one to see
N ice and kind but cheeky too
T ime we had in the submarine
A nd sparkling gems in the sea
S till Lego pieces at the bottom we could see
T ime we go and pick them up
I n the sea, we go
C ome back up to the land

F un times we had
R ight here with this monster
A nd times we cried
N aughty, kind and fabulous are words that describe you
T hinking of your after many years
I will miss you
C ome back soon.

Kianna Pabari (11)
Buxlow Preparatory School, Wembley

Monsters Play At Night

He is slimy, green, sticky and round
When he wakes he makes a sound
Put pat, put pat on the floor
Up the walls and down the door
In the dark with no one in sight
At a secret place, they play all night
Monster tag, stuck in the slime, hide in the shadow
Running around with hid friends until tomorrow
You can see their arms and feet
Behind the trees and under the seats
However, the fun is nearly over
Because the morning sun will soon take over
They say goodbye and quickly walk home
Pit pat, pit pat, with a trail next to the gnome.

Megu Mizuno (7)
Buxlow Preparatory School, Wembley

The Shape-Shifting Beast

Beware at night
When you are in bed
For the shape-shifting beast lurks
His name is Ted
He appears as anything, he has a real look
He is drawn as many things
You can see in a book
He isn't at all friendly
He just wants to eat
But luckily the beast does not eat meat
Unfortunately, he has a craving for haunting
So if you see him at your house
You'll find it quite daunting
So heed these warnings and if you don't
I, the shape-shifting beast,
Will make sure you regret it.

Raihan Ahmed (10)
Buxlow Preparatory School, Wembley

Beware, The Monster Is Coming

Nothing can be finer
Than the Fluffy Diviner

Who runs after your chocolate
Like a baby devil

"Hey dude," he says
"What's for supper today?"

"What do you want thief?" I snarled,
"Oh no,
My chocolate's gone missing today,
It was that thieving devil,
You know what,
He needs a name,
What about Ned, I say!"
"No," says Mum. "What about a nice chocolate name like Orangejet...?"

Noor Al-Zahra Al-Saraj (9)
Buxlow Preparatory School, Wembley

Full Moon

The full moon rises I drop to the floor
As my werewolf change begins
My ears grow long
My tail grows out
My mouth grows fangs and grins

Soon my hands become paws
My nails become claws
My feet become two flippers
My nose is a beak
My back has butterfly wings

I hop around the room
I pound my gorilla chest
My whale song I start to sing
And I spin my web
I start to wonder
If I was bitten by more than one thing!

Amelia Khan (11)
Buxlow Preparatory School, Wembley

Monsters Everywhere

There is a monster in the bathroom
A monster behind the door
A monster in the kitchen, lying on the floor
A monster in the cupboard
A monster hard to see
Even a monster trying to haunt me!
And a tiny little monster
That is very, very greedy
There's a monster who's very fluffy
A monster under your feet
And even a monster that really wants to eat you.

Ruth Emma Caraiman (8)
Buxlow Preparatory School, Wembley

Dogzilla!

Whenever Dogzilla awakes
The earth shakes
With fear
Even though he may not be near
If he goes in to stalk
Your bedroom
He will knock down your door
With a boom
One night
He decided to give me a fright
He opened my door
Creeaak...
But unlike what I expected
There was no roar
I looked down
And saw my dog on the floor!

Amelia Campbell (10)
Buxlow Preparatory School, Wembley

The Lizard

The lizard lives in the jungle
He can eat other animals when it goes red
He can put other lizards to bed
He does flips in the trees
The lizard likes the spiky plants with the bees
He throws dead animal bones
The lizard is stronger than an earthquake
He lives in the long grass where the big cats hide
"Grr!"

Eesa Gaffar (7)
Buxlow Preparatory School, Wembley

The Spooky Monster

On the night of Halloween,
Every monster was ready to scream
Spooky came out without a sound.
She may look fluffy and friendly
But she is actually very scary.
She lays out all her yummy sweets
Watching the children's faces fill with glee
But what they didn't know was
That she had a trick up her sleeve...

Tara Razban (7)
Buxlow Preparatory School, Wembley

The Bed Monster

I think I saw a monster
Underneath my bed
His tongue was yellow
And his eye were red

He loves to eat wood
His favourite food
It puts him in
His very best mood

So the lesson is clear
Consider my plight,
Keep buying wood
Or be dinner tonight!

Timi Areoye (9)
Buxlow Preparatory School, Wembley

There Is A Monster Under My Bed!

I thought I saw a monster underneath my bed
His tongue was pink and his eyes were flashing red
I think I saw his mighty white face
And he likes to wink
But not to sink in water
But *shh* don't make a sound
Or the monster will wake up and will come after you.

Sofia Humayun (8)
Buxlow Preparatory School, Wembley

The Lurks Of Venom

In a child's bedroom
There was a monster called Venom
He eats kids that wear denim
He lurks around children's bedrooms
Waiting for the moment that they go to bed
The floor and bed were shaking
He scuttled around
And then the child disappeared…

Danyaal Kirmani (8)
Buxlow Preparatory School, Wembley

The Booger Man

Booger Man gives boogers for free
And booger tea and snot and slime sandwiches
He asks monsters if they like his shiny skin
And all the monsters say, "Yuck!"
Except one said, "I do like your green skin,
But I don't like your slimy snot."

Nasma Nagi Karileamiden (9)
Buxlow Preparatory School, Wembley

Horny Monster In My Room

There's a monster with a horn in my room
He's scary
He eats flowers
He swims like a spiky branch
He's stronger than a thunderstorm
When he vomits he spits thorny slime out
But he never beats me up because he's my friend.

Elias Humayun (7)
Buxlow Preparatory School, Wembley

Playtime For Bloggery

Bloggery comes slithering down the hall,
He really likes to play with my big, bouncy ball,
I hide under my bed, terrified by what I've seen,
I don't know where he came from or where he's been,
Suddenly, he spots me and lets out a cackle,
I shake and shiver as he moves closer,
I see him dragging his shackles,
Poor Bloggery, he's not a terrible monster,
Just someone looking to have some fun,
Not an imposter!
I come out from beneath my bed and pick the ball,
Then I throw it back to him, right down the hall,
Who would have thought
It was just a friend he sought.

Samuel Epworth (9)
Eureka Primary School, Midway

Monsters Beware

I can hear vicious growls from under my bed,
I can see a monster, it turns out red,
I can feel the eyes keeping an eye on me, all four,
I know it's gonna knock down the door,
It has huge feet,
I dare not say a tweet,
Bang! "What's that?" I say, he's acting vicious,
Maybe he thinks I'm delicious?
I look under the bed again, he's gone, phew!
Will he ever come back?

Corey Barrett-Gray (10)
Eureka Primary School, Midway

Who Is Snoring Under The Stairs?

The night has become
Before the day has come
And there is no more sun.
The children slept but without fear,
The weird parents left,
The monster crept but the child has awoken,
"Run! Run!" children said,
The stairs monster has come,
Georgie was isolated with fear
But they weren't,
Crawling back, he was trembling in fear,
Crack! Haha, he fell.

Boglarka Hegedus (10)
Eureka Primary School, Midway

Bogey McBogeyface, The Killer

In the middle of the night,
Bogey McBogey's face gave me a terrible fright,
It was a horrible dream,
He was slimy and green.

And his sharp teeth
Gave a powerful bite,
He had eight eyes,
And he gave me a surprise.

And all that could be heard
Were my repeated cries.

Caolan Devitt (10)
Eureka Primary School, Midway

Mr Smiley Strikes

Mr Smiley sneaks around,
Mr Smiley likes underground,
Mr Smiley is scary
But, as well, he is hairy,
Mr Smiley will sneak up on you at night
Because he might bite,
Once Mr Smiley hides away
You will be safe throughout the day.

Makenzie Tilt (10)
Eureka Primary School, Midway

Ashley The Angel

Fluffy and scruffy, the fun doesn't stop,
Open the door, then out she pops,
Ashley, she's so soft, she feels like a plushie,
Then I heard a loud noise and headed downstairs
Into my back garden,
To my surprise, oh what a sight,
There was Ashely on my bike!
So I asked, "What are you doing?"
She yelled, "Can't you see? I'm trying to ride it you human being!
Teach me, oh, please, teach me, I never did learn,
It would be a great earn!"
And that is Ashley the angel.

Isabella Hill (9)
Georgetown Primary School, Tredegar

Jelly Johnny, The Clumsy Monster

There's a peep under my bed,
"Monsters aren't real," my parents said,
I heard a trip, then a fall,
Those noises drove me up the wall,
I went downstairs
But what I saw gave me a petrifying scare,
A purple, wobbly monster stood right there,
It went towards me and tried to scare me,
I ran around the house, not worrying about waking my little brother up,
It roamed around a bit, feeling confused,
I looked around for a kitchen utensil to use,
But, it was then I realised that the monster was harmless,
The monster was as dumb as can be,
He could barely put one foot in front of the other, as far as I could see,
Tip, tip, tap was all I could hear,
I knew he was quite near,
But, he was quite stupid, that was quite clear,

I thought I was safe from here,
I decided I needed to get it out
But my chances of doing it gave me a bit of doubt,
I was creeping into the cupboard to the baseball bat,
I heard lots of thuds, I was scared until I saw it was my favourite hat,
I tiptoed around the living room and even down the loo,
But then I finally found it, it had broken the TV too!
I whacked it with the guitar and chased it up the stairs,
Then it jumped out the window as if it'd had a nightmare,
I stared at it through the window as it rolled down the hill,
A grin came across my face, me one point, monster nil.

Tilly Jones (10)
Georgetown Primary School, Tredegar

The Tooth Fairy Got Sacked!

The tooth fairy got sacked,
Oh no! What a terrible time,
But we need a new person
But he cannot commit crimes.

Auditions, auditions, auditions,
Who is this going to be?
It is a big, bad monster that is
The naughtiest they can be!

Drill, drill, drill,
Oh, so many teeth,
Falling on the floor
Ready to bequeath.

Glue, glue, glue,
Glueing all the teeth,
Ready for old people to
Chew all their beef.

The tooth monster went home,
Packed his stuff away,
He's coming back tomorrow,
Ready for another day.

Isabella Templer (9)
Georgetown Primary School, Tredegar

The Brexit Monster

He's tall,
He's round,
He dances all over town,
He hides under the bed
Stroking their little heads,
He comes out when you least expect it,
He's even scarier than Brexit,
He comes out at night
And likes to jump in muddy puddles,
Oh no! He's in a struggle,
It looks like
All the fairy lights tangled him up,
Looks like he's stuck!
He then escapes all through the muck,
The children woke up without a hush!

Mia Kerri Smith (10)
Georgetown Primary School, Tredegar

Creepy Mr Monster

Mr Monster gets into trouble,
He is under your bed, spying on you,
He jumps and shouts around all the time,
He wakes up when you're sleeping,
Down in town he steals all the meat
Because he likes to eat everything, even metal,
Anything he can find,
When there is no more he eats fruit,
One day, he might eat you.

Evan Howells (9)
Georgetown Primary School, Tredegar

Greedy Blue

M onsters are lurking in your room,
O utside, monsters creep around,
N asty monsters stealing food,
S lyly into your fridge the monsters go,
T ime by time, monsters creep,
E ager to play,
R umbling noises as they eat,
S pitting out bones that they leave.

Emily Howells (9)
Georgetown Primary School, Tredegar

The Ghastly Ghost

Ghastly ghosts fly silently over vast cities,
Watching all movement,
Ghosts only come out at midnight,
These monsters find their prey
While their future food is sleeping.

All ghosts meet on the Day of the Dead
At the dead of night,
At the dead of the dead,
Watching all,
Seeing all,
Alert of all.

But, be careful not to pass by Ghastly,
The ghastly, ghostly ghost,
Or you will be gone in seconds,
Do you want to know how I know
All about ghosts?
Because I am one.

Rebecca Temple-Masters (10)
Kent College Junior School, Harbledown

My Monster

He looks like a lime with paws for claws
And when he is angry, he looks like an orange.

His eyes are purple when he is happy
But when he is cross, his eyes are like fire!

He doesn't like ice cream nor pineapples too
And sometimes he just drinks pots of red juice.

He likes eating cakes and biscuits too, yum!
He loves eating pizza and hamburgers, whoo!

He is as heavy as an elephant, too heavy by far,
He is more than one tonne, as heavy as a car!

And, when he is out, he breaks the playground
And when he comes home, he breaks all the floor...

But he is not scary, he is really cute,
But sometimes he can scare you a lot.

If you sit on the sofa and he is not there,
Then he suddenly appears in thin air.

And when he sees danger, he's all fully red
And then, when he calms down, he curls up in his bed.

Sometimes he falls asleep for two days,
Or maybe he has gone as he's turned into a ghost!

Liza Molkova (8)
Kent College Junior School, Harbledown

My Bud, Blobbles

My bud, Blobbles
Is my best friend
And if you throw a tea party,
He'll be sure to attend.

He'll eat up all the food
And make a bit of a mess,
But you'll forgive him in the end,
'Cause he really is the best!

My bud, Blobbbles
Is bubbly and blue
And if you give him anything,
He'll give it a right chew!

We'd go to the shops,
He would overspend,
I would be annoyed at him,
But he is my best friend.

Poppy Armstrong (11)
Kent College Junior School, Harbledown

Gobbles, The Floof

Gobbles the flobbles,
Gobbles the floof,
If you mess with Gobbles,
You'll go *poof!*

My pal Gobbles is very nice,
Gobbles smells of apples and out of date rice.
Gobble's wings are crystal and blue,
How he got here? He flew!

Gobbles favourite food is a cherry,
No matter what, he is so merry!
Hooray, hooray, hooray for all,
Hooray for Gobbles, for he is so small!

Katie Wilkinson (10)
Kent College Junior School, Harbledown

The Mysterious Beast

I see a fat beast from the corner of an eye,
He is as fat as a pig but small like a fly.
He is as transparent as glass
But as shocking as lightning!

Look out, here he comes!
Hide while he stumbles along the corridor,
Scream as he gnashes his vast jaws!

Run if you can
As fast as the wind,
While he lurks
Behind you.

Can you survive the monstrous beast...?

Jim Littlechild (7)
Kent College Junior School, Harbledown

The Hot Sauce Monster

Did you know your nightmares
Sometimes come true? Oooh!

Do you like hot sauce?
Because there's a Hot Sauce Monster!

W-w-what did you say?
A Hot Sauce Monster?
Yes!

His head is a fiery chimney,
His hands are made of hot sauce bottles
And he squirts hot sauce in your mouth!
Beware!

Jake Jennings (7)
Kent College Junior School, Harbledown

My Monster

Run from the toxic croc,
It's coming after you,
It'll vaporise your soul
And send you to a black hole
And it will pour acid on you,
From evening to night, it'll hunt for you
And it'll also trick you,
It will shape-shift into something
But you'll never know who!
You will never know if it's coming after you,
It'll swallow you whole
So don't try messing with me
Because it's my monster!
But, once you get to know him,
He is really friendly,
He giggles under my bed
And helps me prank Dad,
He sometimes croaks like a frog
Which makes me laugh so hard every time,
He is greener than a frog,
Spiky as a hedgehog,

Stealthy as a panther
And as tough as a lion,
He has a snake tongue,
He pretends to be a log,
The reason he does all of those things
Is because he's my monster.

Ayan Kazi (7)
Lathom Junior School, East Ham

The Monster's Adventure

Gobbly was eating,
Gobbly thought, *let's run outside with a bun*
Gobbly had a race,
He won because he is fast,
He had dinner after racing,
For dinner, he had pasta,
For dessert, he had pancakes,
Gobbly always does funny dances,
Everyone heard and had a gleam on their face,
Gobbly went to sleep,
The next day, he woke up,
He went outside with his bun,
He saw a girl,
Suddenly, *achoo!*
He roared loud,
To the extent that the Earth started shaking,
The girl jumped in terror,
But the monster left with shame and nothing else.

Sasmeya Jeyatharsan (7)
Lathom Junior School, East Ham

Monster Stomp Roar

He's as funny as a bunny,
His tongue is as long as a hosepipe,
His horns taste like corn,
He's as soft as a pillow,
He's as tall as a giraffe,
His roar is as loud as a lion,
He waddles like a penguin,
He smells like six rotten eggs,
He licks his ice cream like s*lurp! Slurp! Slurp!*
His eyes are as round as wheels,
As he claps, he shrinks into a little ant.
Amego is a funny monster
Who, in the future, wants to become a jester.

Azaan Muhammed (7)
Lathom Junior School, East Ham

Ronaldo's Rally

This is Ronaldo,
He is as hungry as 4000 humans,
If he roars that means he's bored,
Why not stand up and get yourself a lord?
His arms are so sharp
You will feel like you're in a spiky ark,
He will spot food with no fear
Like a bumbling bear,
He is so black and grey,
Your brain will feel like a lion's hair.

Romman Ali (8)
Lathom Junior School, East Ham

The Day I Met A Monster

One night, as I woke up and ran,
Something turned on the fan,
Oh no, there is a little monster who is cheeky,
It is called Cheepy,
The monster is hairy,
But it isn't too scary,
The monster came to school,
He tried to follow every rule,
He made a light,
He gave a fright!

Yaafi Muhamed Kalil (7)
Lathom Junior School, East Ham

The Monster

Last night, I thought I saw a monster,
Her eyes were as big as a ball,
Her mouth as small as a block,
Every night, I cuddle up
And don't think about the monster,
I feel her hands pulling my hands,
Last night, I thought I saw a monster
As I slept quietly underneath the covers.

Azha Aboobucker (8)
Lathom Junior School, East Ham

The Hungry Slitherman

Smelly stinky socks
That pile up in a box
Are the Slitherman's favourite thing to eat,
The worst is meat,
Leaving a trail of slime,
Which slowly turns into grime,
The Slitherman's very stinky
But known as very kingly.

Basit Shazhad (7)
Lathom Junior School, East Ham

My Secret Monster Pet

Every Saturday night, there's a racket under my bed,
It's my pet monster, waiting to be fed,
I get up with a yawn
Because it is three hours 'til dawn!
I open my suitcase and I see a blue glow,
I have to whisper so no one will know,
It's Giggles, my secret monster pet,
She is more interesting than any other pet you'll get.
She's as sweet as candy and fine and dandy.
I crept downstairs as quietly as I could
But I made a *creak* as I stepped on some wood,
Giggles' fur froze with fear
But I could still hear the sound I wanted to hear,
Mum and Dad, snoring away,
I think they had an exhausting day!
I got a basket of food and let her jump in
And then she had a bit of a swim.

Elena Rose Skehan (7)
Richmond Avenue Primary School, Shoeburyness

The Wardrobe Monster

In your big, dark wardrobe, she's always inside,
The monster is really pretty because she's wearing all your clothes and shoes,
This monster is medium height,
If your wardrobe is small, you will find a squashed monster inside,
This monster is as spiky as a lion's tooth in its mouth,
The monster is as nice as a puppy dog in your hands,
This monster is as lovely as your mum,
This monster is multicoloured so she has a pop of colour everywhere,
She will make you blink,
When you open the wardrobe, you see the monster,
She will ask you for tea and then a party inside,
If you want a cuddle, you can cuddle the monster,
Just don't touch her tail because she has spikes.

Maisy Mulligan (7)
Richmond Avenue Primary School, Shoeburyness

The Friendly Monster Under My Bed

Under my bed, I hear a monster,
It's green with spikes,
It's waiting to pounce,
It's as wet as a storm,
It's in front of me,
It said, "Do you want some tea?"
It's filled with happiness,
"Hello, come with me!
Mrs Dell is not the type, I can tell,
Do you want some tea with me?
I live in a pumpkin at Halloween,
Ned is dead, can you see?
He was my friend,
I'm sad like a slug
And happy like a hippo?
Are you called Ned, wait he's dead,
Won't you smile with glee,
I think I want some tea!"

Bethany Rayner (7)
Richmond Avenue Primary School, Shoeburyness

Mr Pumpkin Head Comes For Tea

In your front garden at Halloween,
There is a pumpkin that you can see,
When you're asleep, he takes a peep,
He uncurls his pumpkin and comes for tea,
When it's morning, he makes breakfast for him,
He makes delicious tea for me, jam, bread and cake
For me when I'm in my bed,
When mangoes fall from mango trees,
He gets tangled for ten years,
When it's Halloween, he disappears
And we go to a Miss Disamerei,
She says, "Go over there, but do take care!"
When it's night, it gets foggy
Because Mr Pumpkin Head comes back.

Chaye Franklin (7)
Richmond Avenue Primary School, Shoeburyness

The Blood Dripper

Blood Dripper,
He hides under your bed,
Loves eating children and sucking their blood,
Odd, blue, green,
Poisonous spots on his tummy,
Odd eyeballs that are evil, red and dark,
Does he eat adults?
Yes, he does!
Do you like my scary, hairy monster?
Right now, he is going to eat you!
He snuck into your house at night,
He only sneaks into your house at night,
Eats your fluff and toys and boxes,
Right now, he is hiding under your bed,
Peers out of a speck of dust!

Jack Nicholls (7)
Richmond Avenue Primary School, Shoeburyness

The Scary Monster Under The Bed At Night

Most of the monsters are nice,
One of them is weird,
My monsters are in the real world,
The kind ones,
So, can you be our friend
To the kind ones?
They are too kind for you
And they are like a polar bear,
They're like dinosaurs with their spikes
Because they're like spiky spiders,
They're like spiders in the dark,
They like to climb into kids' beds in the night.

Lily Scrafton (7)
Richmond Avenue Primary School, Shoeburyness

Soky Bob

"I'm Socky, I live under Sid's bed."
In the night, he eats my socks,
Argh! So cute!
Socky is very cute like a kitten,
He is spotty like a dotty Dalmation,
Socky likes being caring to other people,
He's also super-duper cute
And munches and crunches soft, wavy socks,
He is also very fluffy like a soft, squishy pillow,
Also, he's very spotty.

Sidney Davis (7)
Richmond Avenue Primary School, Shoeburyness

Dethisus

H e is climbing on the ceilings
A nd chiming when he comes closer,
L oads of legs like a spider,
L ives on the hottest part of Venus,
O h, was that a spider or a demon spider.
W hales are smaller than him!
E arth is not his planet, it's Venus,
E veryone is scared of him because he is so huge,
N obody survives him!

Frederick Strydom (8)
Richmond Avenue Primary School, Shoeburyness

Smelly Evil

S melly is under your bed to stink the room out,
M e and Smelly are good friends,
E at children's skin,
L ikes to eat chicken nuggets and children,
L oves to eat spicy food,
Y et, he is still my friend.

E vil as a demon,
V ery good monster,
I eat lots of good food,
L ove my monster.

Olly Owens (8)
Richmond Avenue Primary School, Shoeburyness

Snuggling

G lowchie glows when the sky is dark,
L ive with him and you can snuggle,
O n land, he lives so you don't swim,
W ait 'til you see how snuggly he is!
C lamber onto his back and you still snuggle,
H op onto his back and fall asleep!
I magine how much you could snuggle!
E normous snuggles are always the best!

Isla Mayne (7)
Richmond Avenue Primary School, Shoeburyness

The Little Stinky Pants

My monster is a happy little stinky pant,
He is a lonely little chap,
He lives far away,
He has a very small body and very heavy spikes,
He is a very cheeky monster,
Sometimes he sneaks food from the fridge,
He has spikes all over his body,
He is like a crocodile,
He is like a pig,
He is like a mouse,
When he takes a step, it sounds like a bang!

Leah Rudkin (7)
Richmond Avenue Primary School, Shoeburyness

Truipy

There is a monster under my bed,
I can't stand the noise,
His hair goes *foo foo*,
While the cow outside goes, "Moo moo!"
His claws feel like a cactus,
But now I can't sleep on my mattress,
He's coming for me all the time,
Look out, he's about,
He is as galactic with blue, black and purple,
Like the midnight sky.

Helena Reilly (7)
Richmond Avenue Primary School, Shoeburyness

Bone Crusher The Terrible!

Bone Crusher is a bony monster,
He is called that because he eats lots of bones
And you can see his bones,
He is clear white like a ghost,
He hides behind a post,
Don't go back, he will be back
To crush your bones behind your back,
You can hear him crunch,
When you turn, he isn't there,
When you turn back, he's there.

Henry Gibbs (7)
Richmond Avenue Primary School, Shoeburyness

Megagloby

H e is purple, he eats gerbils,
A ll the time he fights in the night,
L azy days will not be allowed,
L ots of days there will be for him,
O n time to fight people,
W hen he fights, it is uneven,
E very day he will say hello,
E verybody scream!
N obody will try to frighten him.

Roi Reeves (7)
Richmond Avenue Primary School, Shoeburyness

T-Shirt Trouble

T-shirt Tim is very slim.
He lives in a hallway in a house,
He sleeps on T-shirts,
At night, he will come and get your best T-shirt
And leave a trail of slime,
He's as fluffy as a new puppy,
He stamps like thunder, *bang*,
He's so silly and very chilly,
He has fourteen eyes and one smiley mouth!

Phoebe Vickers (7)
Richmond Avenue Primary School, Shoeburyness

Scary Melon

M elon is a monster, he creeps down the street,
"**O** h!" says the boy, Melon is after him,
N o, Melon! He ate the boy,
"**S** top!" said someone, Melon didn't listen
T o the man,
"**E** eek!" said the boy again,
"**R** un!" said the man.

Henry James Peek (7)
Richmond Avenue Primary School, Shoeburyness

Ruby The Rainbow Monster

R uby likes rainbow colours,
U p in the sky,
B ig and furry monsters,
Y ummy food in her tummy.

R eally small eyes,
A ll big and furry,
I ntelligent,
N ot small,
B ig and round,
O h so round,
W ow, so pink!

Emily Hayes (8)
Richmond Avenue Primary School, Shoeburyness

Silly Peanut

Greedy Peanut lives under my bed,
She has a house that is shaped like a peanut,
She eats her house,
She's very greedy, that's why she's called Greedy Peanut,
She has twelve eyes,
She has six arms,
She has ten legs,
She has sharp teeth,
She's very fluffy, kind and green.

Maisie-leigh Ann Craven (7)
Richmond Avenue Primary School, Shoeburyness

Monster Trouble

This is Mr Scary, he's super sleepy,
He's tall and colossal,
His body is furry,
He stomps like thunder, *bang!*
He's cuddly like a pillow,
He has four wriggly arms
Which are furrier than ever,
He's as big as a giant panda,
His demon horns make him a devil!

Roody Gregory (8)
Richmond Avenue Primary School, Shoeburyness

My Monster Will Snuggle With You

My monster is cute and cuddly,
Snuggly, spotty, hairy, dirty, scary and weird,
He is following you where you go,
He is scary, hairy and beardy,
He's so cute, gentle, hairy and scary,
Very scary, beardy, weird, bad
And he likes to jump!

Edward Davis (7)
Richmond Avenue Primary School, Shoeburyness

Glowey

G lowey glows at night,
L ives in your house,
O n the darkest night of the year, he comes under your cover,
W hen it is morning, he comes right out,
E ven eats your breakfast,
Y ou will think, no!

Finley Moyser (8)
Richmond Avenue Primary School, Shoeburyness

The Monster Under Your Bed

Stripy sleeps under your bed,
Snoring in the night,
You can hear him roaring,
He will give you quite a fright!

There is a sister, Fuzzy,
She is very pink,
If you want to find her
Look under the kitchen sink!

Amber Queen-Brooks (7)
Richmond Avenue Primary School, Shoeburyness

Spooky Dooky

M onster I see under my bed,
O nly I can see him,
N aughty and slimy,
S lithery like a snake,
T errifying I see he is,
E xtremely spooky and wild,
R eally, only I can see him.

Amelie Ellen Morley (7)
Richmond Avenue Primary School, Shoeburyness

Kitty

K itty is my name, I am a creepy monster,
I walk down the street, watching
T ill everyone is asleep,
T en o'clock, my time to strike,
Y ou'd better watch out, I'm coming.

Maxx Mulligan (7)
Richmond Avenue Primary School, Shoeburyness

Spider

E very time I come out from under the bed,
V ases fall from above onto my head!
I don't know where they are coming from, I cried!
L icking lollipops helps me think about where to hide.

Eliza Grooms (7)
Richmond Avenue Primary School, Shoeburyness

Jeffy

M onster eyes everywhere,
O h no!
N o friends here,
S o long,
T ry to escape but the door is locked,
E ek! Scary and hairy!
R ed and more colours of skin.

Tommy Heal (7)
Richmond Avenue Primary School, Shoeburyness

The Monster Who Likes Meat

This monster is Ronaldo,
He likes to eat meat,
He likes cows and sheep,
He is spiky and very colourful
And is very friendly,
When you are sleeping
He will get in bed with you!

Teddy Rutt (8)
Richmond Avenue Primary School, Shoeburyness

Globy Floyd

G lobly is very brave and friendly,
L oud and super cute,
O ld he is, over 200 years,
B lobby and very soggy,
Y oghurt-textured skin, slimy and green.

Daniel Floyd (7)
Richmond Avenue Primary School, Shoeburyness

Billion Yellow Eyes Monster

E vil, wild and wicked monster,
V ery spiky tail and tummy,
I eat children and slugs and other little monsters,
L ives in a cave, he has a billion eyes to see.

Harley Adams (7)
Richmond Avenue Primary School, Shoeburyness

Slimey

S limey loves eating toes,
L ikes eating rubbish too,
I love eating chicken,
M y monster is bad,
E vil monster,
Y ay, he is so dirty.

Mason Osborne (7)
Richmond Avenue Primary School, Shoeburyness

Matthew

M y monster
A lways jokes,
T all as the sky,
T eeth to crunch,
H uge, big belly,
E xcited for football,
W arm cuddles.

Matthew Bannister (7)
Richmond Avenue Primary School, Shoeburyness

Poetry Monsters - Fangtastic Poets

Spiky

E very night, he eats children in the dark,
V ile little monster,
I f you see him, he will eat you,
L ittle monster sees people and eats them all.

Anna Rayner (7)
Richmond Avenue Primary School, Shoeburyness

All About Happy Chappy

H e has eight wiggly arms
A nd is as hungry as a shark,
P erfect, smooth tongue,
P rickly tail,
Y ucky, gross, prickly fingers.

Luqa James (8)
Richmond Avenue Primary School, Shoeburyness

Jef

He is as spotty as a cheetah,
He likes to be as mean as a lion,
He is as mean as a brain,
He is as large as a pumpkin,
He growls when someone winds him up.

Summer Nunn (8)
Richmond Avenue Primary School, Shoeburyness

Noodles

Noodles sleeps on top of you,
Then I shout, "Cool!"
Noodles screams
Whilst I eat ice cream,
Noodles likes to bike,
I like to fly a kite!

Ava-Mai Westaway (6)
Richmond Avenue Primary School, Shoeburyness

My Monster

I was making a monster in my lab room,
Mixing the ingredients, it would be ready soon,
A sprinkle of this and a sprinkle of that,
Some fluff, some hair, two wings of a bat,
I counted to five
And it popped alive,
It had sunset wings, midnight sky feet,
The nicest monster you would ever meet,
"Hi, I'm Earth, did you make me?"
"Yes, I'm Martha and I'm so happy!"
Next, I asked, "What can you do?"
Then he said, "I can shape-shift for you!"
Earth changed into a dog, a fish and a cat,
A hamster, a guinea pig and then to a rat,
We had a good laugh
When he changed into me and back,
He moved in with me and we became good friends
And now this poem has come to an end.

Martha Faye Valentine Appleby (9)
Ripponden Junior & Infant School, Ripponden

Sunrise

"Heatwave, Heatwave, Heatwave," she said,
"She won't watch me in my bed!"
Her sister said, "Come on you fool,
Or we'll be late for school!"

As they were driving to school,
Her sister was still calling her a fool,
She thought she caught a glimpse of Heatwave,
With a slave!

"Heatwave, Heatwave, Heatwave," he said,
"She won't watch me in my bed,"
He thought *this Heatwave thing's for fools*,
I better get to school!

When he was walking to school,
Looking all cool,
He saw Heatwave come out of her cave,
When they both got to school,
He looked very cool,
Though she too wasn't cool.

At home, he was forced to go

To the 'fool's' house with his pet mouse,
Soon, it was time for bed,
The time they should dread,
For, the next day, they were found.

Isla Alice Vevers (10) & Maya Rose Willacy
Ripponden Junior & Infant School, Ripponden

Mick, My Monster!

Well, Mick is actually a girl,
She's shy but very loud,
But here's the problem, I lost her, LOL,
I looked back and she was nowhere,
If you see her by any chance?
She always wears a hat and has two odd flower horns,
She always smells fishy and Mick is also fat
And big!
She badly screams like a girl,
Mick has long, green nails, and snot running down her,
When Mick speaks, she spits on everything!
Very long, pointy ears,
She'll gobble you up if you're in sight,
She might even roast you for tea!
Yep, that could be you!
Call XXX-XXX-XXX-XX if you see her,
That's my number!
A big mouth, blue eyes,

Hairy chinny chin chin,
Beware, she farts every single day!

Annabella Brook (10)
Ripponden Junior & Infant School, Ripponden

Look Out For Mr Snufflebottom

Whenever you're about to play,
Mr Snufflebottom will barge in and say,
"I want to play with someone!"
And just because he smelt that bad
No one wanted to play with him
Which made him very sad.

Even when he goes to the city,
People will shout, "Look out for Mr Snufflebottom!"
So, he left with a pout,
When he gets home, he'll feel depressed,
Lie down and have a rest.

So, if you are outside, about to play
And you see Mr Snufflebottom shout, "Good day!"
When he comes over, why don't you ask,
"Hey, Mr Snufflebottom, do you want to play?"
And he will quickly say, "Hooray!"

Amelie Wallwork (10)
Ripponden Junior & Infant School, Ripponden

The Monster Dog Poem

Once there was a monster, she was called Miss Fluffy,
She acted like a dog but jumped like a frog,
But don't mind her, she is silly,
She can fly like a cloud but you better watch out,
She is spotty and she is funny,
She is gentle but she is mental,
She is magical and she is pretty cheeky,
She is colourful and she is beautiful,
She is big and she is a pig,
She is loud and she is proud of her jumps,
She is very good and she is very happy,
She is red, orange, yellow, green, blue and pink and purple,
She is good at running and jumping,
She is very fun to play with,
She is good at singing and dancing,
I like my monster so much!

Alisha Whitelaw (9)
Ripponden Junior & Infant School, Ripponden

Monster Mania

My monster lives in Slug Mania next to Pluto,
This little fella is not very nice,
His flesh is as cold as ice,
I met a monster at his house
And he was called Slug Stinger,
Slug Stinger had Medusa hair
And was as strong as a grizzly bear,
He went out to the shop
But, then, somebody said, "Stop!"
So, Stinger walked off to the beach,
Then someone said, "Would you like a peach?"
Someone gave him a freeze ray
And he walked and did not pay.
He took his soggy sunglasses off
And it made people cough,
Slug Stinger went home and ate some tea
And then he said, "Yummy!"

Willow Jennings (10)
Ripponden Junior & Infant School, Ripponden

Terry The T-Rex

In my history class,
Learning about a monster,
We've just had a massive smash,
Where the monsters have gone forever.
Terry the T-rex is incredibly tall,
No smaller than a block of flats,
He's even hungrier than Paul,
A country of people should do!
His nails have got grime,
Incredibly stinky too,
His teeth are much bigger than mine
And could easily chomp through a tree!
I wouldn't want to meet Terry,
Even though he's quite cool,
He isn't as sweet as a berry,
So, I'm not sure if he'd like me either.

Gwynneth Harrison-Walker (11)
Ripponden Junior & Infant School, Ripponden

Fred

I was in my bed,
When I saw a monster called Fred,
He was large, black and scary
And he was very hairy,
His horns were like pins
And he smelt like our bins,
His eyes were like the sky at night,
I was shivering with fright!
I leapt out of bed,
But my feet were like lead,
I reached for the light,
Which flickered on white and bright.
I ran to my mum and dad,
My dad had disappeared and I felt very sad,
The monster drew closer,
We hid behind a poster,
We heard his footsteps and saw his feet,
Who were we about to meet?

Ben Lucas Hillcoat (8)
Ripponden Junior & Infant School, Ripponden

The Not-So Scary Monster (Or So I Thought)

When I saw it, my face went blank,
It felt as if I was walking the plank,
I ran into my room drowned with fear,
Rolling down my cheek was a big, fat tear.

The monster shouted with a mighty roar,
It came into my house and smashed down my door,
It gave me a glare I could never forget,
Then, from his pockets, he pulled out a tea set.

At first, I thought it was fun and games,
But, as soon as I touched it, it burst into flames,
It scorched my hand and I had to scream,
That was when I woke up from a monstrous dream.

George Hughes (10)
Ripponden Junior & Infant School, Ripponden

The Night-Time Monster

Are there monsters in my head?
Is there a monster under my bed?

Is it real?
Is it really real?
Hopefully, it doesn't think of me as a tasty meal.

Is it nice?
Does it only eat mice?
Or is it a different story completely?

Wait, there is a shadow shining on my door,
I just can't ignore
The things being thrown on my floor!
Bang!
What was that?
I heard a low cry from under my bed,
I had a look but it was all in my head.

Eryn Ideson-Sharp (11)
Ripponden Junior & Infant School, Ripponden

Pretend

Some monsters like you to hear their roars,
Some monsters have very sharp claws,
Some have very furry paws
And some monsters have gigantic jaws,
But this monster didn't want to be scary and loud,
She didn't want to stand out in the crowd,
She wanted to be everybody's friend,
This monster was called Pretend,
She was really very shy,
For she was living a lie,
She was assumed to be scary and tough,
When really, it was all one big bluff.

Sophie Oxley (9)
Ripponden Junior & Infant School, Ripponden

Birt's Burps

It's Birt, it's Birt, it's Burping Birt,
Burping Birt burping mushy peas and cheese,
Fishy trouts and sprouts around me,
Oh, I wish that I could be far away,
Far away from Birt, you see!
Sausage with stuffing made with sage,
Smelly fish with a Chinese dish,
Burping Birt burping bacon crisps and chips!
Oh, mushy peas and cheese,
Trouts and sprouts,
Smelly fish and Chinese,
How I wish I could be faraway from these!

Else Hughes (8)
Ripponden Junior & Infant School, Ripponden

The Monster Under The Bed

He's small, he's slimy,
He's the monster under the bed,
His name is Pulba and he lives
Under a little boy's bed,
He is green and slimy,
He has massive feet,
They are thirty centimetres long,
He has cat eyes and a dog nose,
He has two arms just like octopus tentacles,
His horns are made of fingernails,
So, if there is something strange in your room,
Remember Pulba, especially if you're a young boy.

Poppy Sowden (9)
Ripponden Junior & Infant School, Ripponden

If I Had A Monster

If I had a monster
He would be called Cilot,
When he is older, he will want to be a pilot,
He will be two,
I would think he was turning cuckoo,
He would pound like a dog
But sound like a frog,
Though he definitely couldn't leap,
He could still keep,
Some people would hate him,
But they would say he's good for bait,
He would always be late,
For things I love,
Like when I was going to buy a dove.

Katie Huckauf (9)
Ripponden Junior & Infant School, Ripponden

The Tentacle Monster

When you're climbing up the stairs,
He likes to catch you unawares.
His tentacles are slimy and green,
he's the strangest thing you've ever seen.
Don't be frightened, no need to run,
All he wants is to have some fun.
His tentacles will reach out to tickle,
he's not scary, he will make you giggle.
So, next time you're climbing up the stairs,
He'll be behind you, but don't be scared!

Freya Elizabeth Gatehouse (9)
Ripponden Junior & Infant School, Ripponden

The Golden Deadly Peacock

If you ever see a golden peacock,
Run, scream,
It is deadly,
One night was a strange night
For a girl named Emily,
She was just a normal girl
But one night was not normal for her,
She was walking in the woods,
A golden peacock stood behind a tree,
She went to stroke it,
Its deadly feathers fanned out,
In the blink of an eye... she turned, haunted.

Gioia Giardina (8)
Ripponden Junior & Infant School, Ripponden

Nice Dreams Monster

There is a monster that gives you nice dreams,
It can't be found on the streets,
It can't be found in the woods,
It is my monster,
It is in my head!
She is a girl, her name is Verocious Violet!
She is only eight years old,
She lives in Monster Town,
She has a friend called Freya,
She is a girl and is thoughtful.

Charlotte Mae Wood (8)
Ripponden Junior & Infant School, Ripponden

Our Monster

Our monster lives under the ice,
Our monster is very nice,
Our monster is big and scary,
Our monster is also hairy,
Our monster wears a flower,
Our monster has great power,
Our monster is rather red,
Our monster sleeps on a huge bed,
Our monster is our pet,
Though we haven't met her yet.

Poppy Laws (10) & Lucy Hood (10)
Ripponden Junior & Infant School, Ripponden

My Monster Poem

Has anyone seen my monster?
He might have a large sense of humour!
It might be black and spiky,
He will most likely rip up the sofa.

- **V** icious,
- **E** normous,
- **N** aughty,
- **O** utrageous,
- **M** uscular.

Evan Jacob Leyland (9)
Ripponden Junior & Infant School, Ripponden

Claude

His name is Claude,
He cheers me up when I am bored,
He is very hairy,
Some find him scary,
He is spiky but he is really not mean,
He is my best friend!

Cameron William Snape (9)
Ripponden Junior & Infant School, Ripponden

The Bony Husk 2.0

He roams in the night,
He likes to bring the fright,
Make sure you're tucked up tight.

He has a cage,
No one knows his age,
He has some boiling bubbles,
But he makes tons of trouble.

If you hear his growl,
He's on the prowl,
Run as fast as you can,
Of this Bony Monster, you won't be a fan,
His claws won't hurt you,
It'll kill you in his cage,
He has spikes that can kill you
When he's in a rage!

Kenny Jenkins (9)
Tai Education Centre, Penygraig

The Lovable Linker

She hovers over the grass like a big, slimy sloth,
As well as that she needs to pose,
A scary scale is on her big, fat back,
She feels like a venomous bat
But fouler!
You don't want to go near her,
Otherwise, she will destroy you for good,
She feels like a pug,
She really needs a hug!
When you look at her, she starts to grow,
When you stare at her, she shoots her bow.

Jack Swales (9)
Tai Education Centre, Penygraig

The Kid Gobbler

He eats kids so he can fly,
All the children start to cry,
Smells like a sewer
Around the streets he tours,
He growls and stomps down the street
When all are asleep,
The Kid Gobbler is gross, gory, gloomy and green,
Trick or treat, Happy Halloween!

Kian Davies (10)
Tai Education Centre, Penygraig

Lovely Bubbles

This monster is called Bubbles,
He is as fluffy as a bunny,
As cute as a puppy,
As funny as a jelly.

Cameron Williams (10)
Tai Education Centre, Penygraig

Little Naughty Flurple

Flurple's smelly naughty breath filled the room with a pong,
He shape-shifted into the choir and broke into song.
Flurple's fangs poke out of his mouth,
He is as hairy as a dog.
Flurple's naughty skills are really quite impressive,
But this is not all of Flurple's silly message.
Flurple is not that mean,
He has one eye and really likes flies.
He looks weird,
But he's really friendly.
Now here's one thing I need to tell you:
Please be Flurple's friend!

Lottie Watson (7)
Uffculme Primary School, Uffculme

Horror Horns

M y monster roams through the evil night, as hungry as a dinosaur.
O n that night, he will be waiting for children's snores.
N othing will stop my monster's feast, else his feet will stink.
S ay a word, no time to sleep, don't talk, don't 'yeek!'
T ime for Horror Horns to come to play, but you don't want him to stay!
"E ek!" you'll say when Horror Horns comes your way.
R eally think you won't get bitten? Well, Horror Horns' spikes you'll feel!
S ay, "Horror Horns" and that will be it; you'll get bitten.

P lay 'Snake-alike', he'll turn into a snake as green as can be!
O h, the monster's feet buzz. Horror Horns needs some sleep.
E ating in the night with Horror Horns, flying and swimming,
M y monster feels the beat like a dancer on stage, as graceful as could be!

Will you be his friend?
We'll start moving to the beat!

Maisy Whitehead (7)
Uffculme Primary School, Uffculme

Fangs!

M y monster is as hungry as a T-rex.
O ne night, Fangs was stomping.
N ot only will he bite, but he will also fight.
S o beware!
T otally friendly, he is just hungry.
E ek! Horror
R ight from the street.

P lay all day till Fangs comes.
O h, let Fangs sleep.
E ating in the night, *crunch, crunch,*
M y monster is as spiky as ten cactuses!

Alfie Craig Collins (7)
Uffculme Primary School, Uffculme

I Am Furry Eyes

I am furry, fluffy
And I am a blue monster
I become good friends with a boy
Named Roy
I lived in a wooden den
Then got chased by some scary men
Then went back to my den
And saw my pet hen named Ben!
I eat my food
Then spit it out again
I talk to myself
I then go to bed
I wake up in the morning
Then get dressed
I go out again
And hope I don't mess up again!

Zac Matthews (8)
Uffculme Primary School, Uffculme

Dave, The Cheeky Monster

Dave is cheeky,
He's eating cake,
The one I just baked.
He's covering the jar in slime,
He's going to play outside,
To play by the pond.
He slipped over and fell in the pond,
He can't swim,
And he is small.
He will fit in my fishing net.
He is a monkey,
Oh, Dave.
Dave has gone to sleep,
And now he's snoring.
People think he's boring!

Flora Copland (8)
Uffculme Primary School, Uffculme

Little Squiggle Monster

Meet Squiggle...

His eyes look like fireballs,
His teeth are really sharp,
He can make a wall of fire with a tiny spark.

He is as big as a house,
He is as dangerous as barbed wire,
His eyes look just like balls of fire.

He gives you a really big fright,
His eyes are as red as fire,
He likes to find people in the night and eat them in one bite.

Kara Kneale (8)
Uffculme Primary School, Uffculme

The Noisy Night

What is that noise?
It is coming from under the toy box.
What is that noise?
Let's go and see.
What is that noise?
I can see something.
What is that creature?
So big and pink.
What could it be?
Let's see...
Oh, it is Sammy!
He was snoring in the box.
Silly me, I thought it was a monster.
It is quiet now,
Oh, what a noisy night!

Laurie Poynton (7)
Uffculme Primary School, Uffculme

Strong

Strong was scary,
But really hairy
And the opposite of a fairy.
Strong was black,
A complete maniac!
Strong was strong
And always said, "Pong!"
He bought a tail,
From a sale.
Strong threw a pan,
At a man
And made him fall
Into a stall!
He had lots of bumps
That looked like lots of thumps.
I like Strong.

Jack Bolt (8)
Uffculme Primary School, Uffculme

Riddle McTiddle

M onsters lurk through your room
O ver there, monsters are everywhere
N ever go near those monsters
S ee for yourself, monsters are everywhere
T ime is running out, quick, get those monsters out; especially the spiky, dirty and slimy ones!
E very day monsters stay
R iding and roaming, monsters are everywhere!

Amelia Emma Anne Hanley (7)
Uffculme Primary School, Uffculme

Army Gecko

A rmy Gecko is brave.
R anks 10,000.
M ucky, he does not care.
Y o-yos are his best thing.

G reen is his colour.
"E ek," he does not say.
C amo makes him green.
K omodo dragons are his friends.
O ne is his lucky number.

Harry Johnson (8)
Uffculme Primary School, Uffculme

My Monster

Fluf is fluffy,
He likes to explore
And always snores.
Fluf sleeps in my bed,
His owner is Ted,
He gets mighty hot,
I'm not surprised!
He has hair
Like a polar bear,
Now it comes to bed,
Fluf and Ted need to go to bed.
So goodnight
You lot reading, sleep tight.

Kian Hector (8)
Uffculme Primary School, Uffculme

Monsters

He can feel and sense
He's got 1,000 sharp golden spikes on his feet.
He is bigger than two double-decker buses.
His hair is as silent as two big cats hunting.
His spikes are as loud as twigs cracking.
His voice is as horrible as two eagles shouting.

His name is Snotty.

Alyssia Irene Hayes (7)
Uffculme Primary School, Uffculme

Rad Is Mad!

This is Rad
And he is mad,
The next day there was a flood
Full of very red blood,
He thought he should
Be very good,
Rad was spotty
And used a potty,
Rad had a hog
Who was called Dog,
And this is how Rad
Became very mad!

Jagoda Kramarz (8)
Uffculme Primary School, Uffculme

Mr Spiky

Some monsters are scary.
Some monsters are not scary.
No monsters are allowed!
The sun is not shining in the sky.
Tears drop when you see a monster.
"Eek!" You are scared.
Run quickly,
The sun isn't shining in the village!

Louis Taylor (7)
Uffculme Primary School, Uffculme

Scary Monster

My monster has eyes as big as an animal,
My monster is as hungry as a shark,
My monster is as stinky as a slug,
When it is night, my monster goes under beds and scares kids.
My monster is as slow as a worm,
My monster roams in the night.

Wiktoria Bylicka (7)
Uffculme Primary School, Uffculme

My Monster

There's a monster under my bed
I can see his head,
I try to sleep at night
But he gives me quite a fright!
His hair
Is quite a scare,
I can hear burping
From the slurping
Of juice.
His nail
Is very pale...

Harley Carreau (8)
Uffculme Primary School, Uffculme

Fang Song

When you are sleeping, you can taste that horribleness.

You can feel that sharpness on your little toes.
You can see its eye is glowing in the dark.

You would think it might choose you,
And it might gobble you up. Oh yes!

Freya C H Mills (7)
Uffculme Primary School, Uffculme

Monster Poem

M y monster is as hungry as 100 sharks.
O nly Buster has an orange tummy.
N oisy as a bus.
S illy as a monkey.
T all as a human.
E veryone's scared!
R eally scary, deadly Buster.

Maddox Welch (7)
Uffculme Primary School, Uffculme

Googly

Googly's spikes are as big as a rhino's horn
Googly's eyes go back and forward in the wind
Shsh go Googly's eyes in the wind
His teeth are as big as an elephant's tusk
Googly is as hard as a rhino.

Summer Freeman (7)
Uffculme Primary School, Uffculme

Lightning Go

This is Lightning,
He is as hungry as a ferocious lion
His belly is as big as the classroom
He is as hungry as a rhino and as cool as me.
Yeah!
My monster is as ugly as his school.

Will you be his friend?

Alfie Ibbitson (7)
Uffculme Primary School, Uffculme

Smolic Long's Monster

A little monster goes into your home
Under your bed
He never goes to Ted
He's cute
But he might make you puke!
He lives in a palace
But he does not like Alice
He likes chairs
But not pears.

Alfie Tarr (8)
Uffculme Primary School, Uffculme

Gliding Gecko

M ightily fast
O bedient monster
N ight-flyer
S ilent like a mouse.
T ired in the day
E xercise is important to him.
R umbling footsteps. Will you be his friend?

Jacob Jaffri (8)
Uffculme Primary School, Uffculme

The Ugly Monster Story

Once, there was a monster
His name was Jaws
He was very snappy
With his fur that was blue
He was very cheeky
Because he snuck
Under my bed
And crunched his snacks
With his sharp claws.

Kayla Pike (8)
Uffculme Primary School, Uffculme

Joey

I know a monster who's called Joey
And has a friend called Zoey.
When I go up to him, he snaps
And taps
Me on the back.
I don't know why,
But he gives me a fright
And he has a kite.

Taylor Lindsell (8)
Uffculme Primary School, Uffculme

Yucky

Yucky eats people and animals from every country in the world
Very strong and its teeth are scary.

My monster eats yucky food.
My monster is a kind, happy monster.
My monster's eyes are scary!

Declan Hutchings (7)
Uffculme Primary School, Uffculme

There's A Monster Under Bed

I can see a monster
And he hides
Under my bed
At night.
Hear him snore
Like a pig.
When he's asleep
I try
And pull
Pull him out
But
He's too
Big!

Isaac Ronnie Tanner (8)
Uffculme Primary School, Uffculme

No Name Eats Names

No Name is scary
And hairy,
He has a tail
That is pale,
Then he threw a nail
At his tail!
He has three horns
That are covered in thorns,
He is small
And can crawl.

Fyfe Milby (8)
Uffculme Primary School, Uffculme

Fred

My monster is as strong as a lion.
My monster's spikes are as sharp as knives.
My monster is as hairy as a tiger.
My monster has an eye that can look one mile.

Mike Orchard (7)
Uffculme Primary School, Uffculme

Monster Molly

Monster Molly,
Was very jolly
And she lived in holly.
She was so cute,
She put me on mute.
Her favourite food is a chip,
And she puts it in a dip.

Emilie Matthews (9)
Uffculme Primary School, Uffculme

Bob

Bob is fluffy
And scruffy.
His eyes are round like footballs.
Down in his hole
There is a mole.
They go for a stroll
Out of the hole!

Koby Ware (8)
Uffculme Primary School, Uffculme

Stinky Lucy

S he finds little people at a creepy time, she's like a vampire.
T he children are really frightened.
I n the middle of the black night, they have bad, bad dreams.
N obody knows what she looks like,
K icking everything in her way.
Y ou have to run away!

L ucy is super smelly with flies twirling around her hair. *Buzz... buzz... buzz.*
U nder her green-as-a-frog dress, there is pink dirty skin.
C an you hear her loud stomping at night? *Bam... bam... bam.*
Y ou can get scratched by Lucy's claws sharp as a shark's teeth...

Agata Julianna Bolejko (6)
Victoria Road Primary School, Ashford

YOUNG WRITERS INFORMATION

We hope you have enjoyed reading this book – and that you will continue to in the coming years.

If you're a young writer who enjoys reading and creative writing, or the parent of an enthusiastic poet or story writer, do visit our website **www.youngwriters.co.uk**. Here you will find free competitions, workshops and games, as well as recommended reads, a poetry glossary and our blog. There's lots to keep budding writers motivated to write!

If you would like to order further copies of this book, or any of our other titles, then please give us a call or order via your online account.

Young Writers
Remus House
Coltsfoot Drive
Peterborough
PE2 9BF
(01733) 890066
info@youngwriters.co.uk

Join in the conversation!
Tips, news, giveaways and much more!

 YoungWritersUK @YoungWritersCW